P9-DCL-812

THOMAS & FRIENDS

THOMAS AND THE DINOSAUR

Illustrated by Tom LaPadula

🌷 A GOLDEN BOOK • NEW YORK

Thomas the Tank Engine & Friends™

CREATED BY BRITT ALLCROFT

Based on The Railway Series by The Reverend W Awdry.
© 2000, 2015 Gullane (Thomas) LLC.
Thomas the Tank Engine & Friends and Thomas & Friends are trademarks of Gullane (Thomas) Limited.
HIT and the HIT Entertainment logo are trademarks of HIT Entertainment Limited.
All rights reserved. Published in the United States by Golden Books, an imprint of Random House Children's
Books, a division of Random House LLC, 1745 Broadway, New York, NY 10019, and in Canada by Random
House of Canada Limited, Toronto, Penguin Random House Companies. Adapted from *Thomas and the Dinosaur*
by Christopher Awdry, originally published in Great Britain in 1997 by Reed Books Children's Publishing.
Subsequently published in different form by Random House Children's Books, New York, in 2000. Golden Books, A
Golden Book, A Little Golden Book, the G colophon, and the distinctive gold spine are registered trademarks of
Random House LLC.
ISBN 978-0-553-49681-9 (trade) — ISBN 978-0-553-49682-6 (ebook)
randomhousekids.com
www.thomasandfriends.com
Printed in the United States of America
10

Random House Children's Books supports the First Amendment and celebrates the right to read.

One day, Percy rushed into the Shed.
"I saw a monster in the forest!" he said.
"What's a monster?" Thomas asked.
"Monsters are very big animals with very big teeth," Percy answered. "And they eat engines!"

Thomas was a little bit scared to go near the forest, but he had work to do.

Suddenly, he saw a very big animal with very big teeth.

"Monster!" Thomas shouted as he raced back to tell Percy.

"I saw it!" Thomas said with a shudder.
"The monster?" Percy asked.
"Yes!" Thomas replied. "But I got away!"

Just then, Sir Topham Hatt came into the Shed.

"Thomas," he said, "I need you to bring a special load from the forest."

Now Thomas was really worried. What if he met up with the monster again?

Slowly, slowly, Thomas puffed back to the
forest with his driver.

Through the trees, Thomas again saw that
very big animal with the very big teeth.

"Monster!" he shouted to his driver.

"That's not a monster," the driver said. "That's just a model of a dinosaur."

"What's a dinosaur?" Thomas asked him.

"Dinosaurs were animals that lived a long, *long* time ago," the driver explained. "This is a model for Sodor's new Dinosaur Park."

Thomas chugged a little closer and saw that his driver was right.

Soon, Harold the Helicopter arrived to lift the dinosaur.

Then some workers guided Harold as he carefully lowered the model onto Thomas' flatbed.

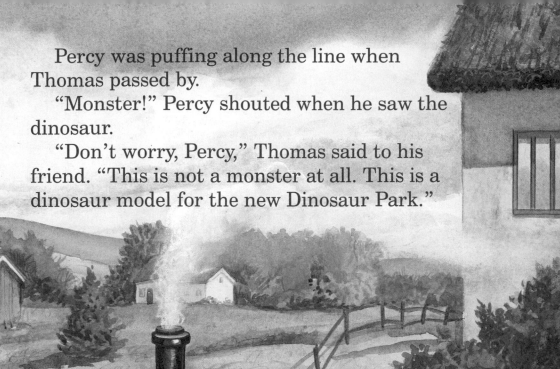

Percy was puffing along the line when Thomas passed by.

"Monster!" Percy shouted when he saw the dinosaur.

"Don't worry, Percy," Thomas said to his friend. "This is not a monster at all. This is a dinosaur model for the new Dinosaur Park."

Thomas was very proud to be carrying the
dinosaur model.

He rolled past the schoolyard with the
dinosaur, and the children waved with
excitement.

"*Peep! Peep!*" Thomas called.

Finally, Thomas reached the Dinosaur Park. Sir Topham Hatt met him there. "Good work, Thomas," Sir Hatt said. "You've been Very Useful today!"

The dinosaur was placed in a spot where everyone could see it, from inside the park and out. And every time he passed by, Thomas smiled and gave a special *"Peep! Peep!"*